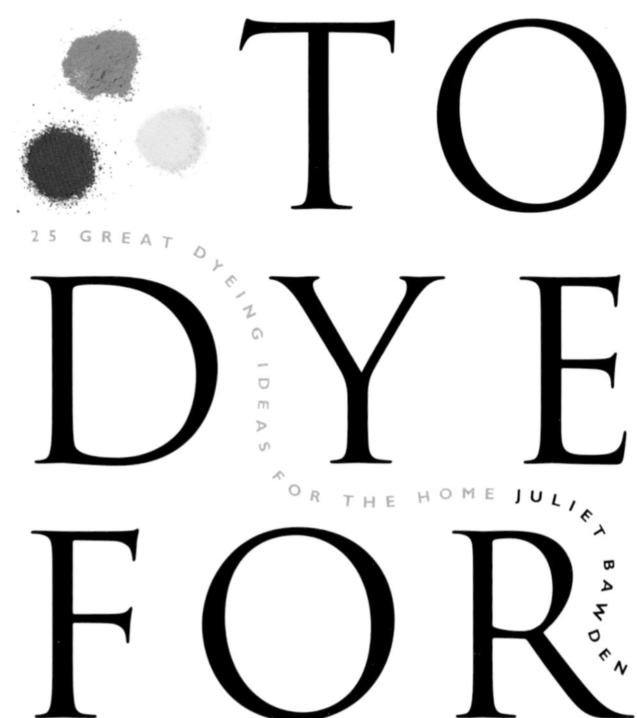
TO
DYE
FOR
25 GREAT DYEING IDEAS FOR THE HOME
JULIET BAWDEN

TO DYE FOR

25 GREAT DYEING IDEAS FOR THE HOME

JULIET BAWDEN

The Overlook Press
Woodstock • New York

DEDICATION

This book is dedicated to Labeena Ishaque, my wonderful assistant, for all her hard work over the last two years, and wishing her all success in the future.

ACKNOWLEDGMENT

As the author, it is my name which goes on the cover of this book but it has been produced by a team of people to whom I give my thanks for all their hard work – my editor Venetia Penfold, Marie-Louise Avery and Martin Klejnowski for stunning photography, DWN's Katrina Dallamore and Daniel Duke for art direction and finally, Claudia Passera. Thank you to the 6th Streatham Girl Guide troop for help with tie dyeing: Anna Race, Jolanta Shrowiak, Amy-Louise Moyes, Annabelle Woods, Alex Pullin, Alex Towers.

First published in the United States in 1997 by
Thr Overlook Press, Peter Mayer Publishers, Inc.
Lewis Hollow Road
Woodstock, New York 12498

Library of Congress Cataloging-in-Publication Data

Bawden, Juliet
To dye for: 25 great dyeing ideas for the home / Juliet Bawden
p. cm.
1. Dyes and Dyeing, Domestic. 2. Color in textile crafts. I Title
TT853.B39 1997 667 3-dc21 96-39666 CIP

ISBN 0-87951-785-9

Printed in Hong Kong

First American Edition
2 4 6 8 9 7 5 3 1

Styled photography by Marie-Louise Avery
Cut-out and flat-shot photography by Martin Klejnowski
Copy-edited by Caroline Bingham

CONTENTS

INTRODUCTION 6
A BRIEF HISTORY OF DYEING 7

MATERIALS & TECHNIQUES
MATERIALS 10
  TYPES OF DYES 10
  EQUIPMENT 12
  FABRIC 12
TECHNIQUES 16
  GETTING STARTED 16
  USING DIFFERENT DYES 16
  CREATING PATTERNS 18
  COLOR 24

LIVING SPACES
PATCHWORK THROW 28
VELVET PILLOWS 30
DIRECTOR'S CHAIR 32
GAUZE CURTAINS 34
SOFA THROW 38
DAISIES UNDERFOOT 40
CHEST OF DRAWERS 42
TAB CURTAINS 44
EMBROIDERED PILLOWS 48

BEDROOMS
DUVET COVER & PILLOWCASES 52
TERRIFIC TOWELS 54
DOTTY HAT BOXES 56
RUSTIC STOOL 60
TRUE BLUE PILLOWS 62
MINIATURE CHEST 64
GORGEOUS GINGHAM 66
WOOLEN MAT 70

ACCESSORIES
LOVELY LINEN 74
WRAPPING PAPER 76
PICTURE FRAMES 78
STORAGE BOXES 82
GINGHAM TABLECLOTH 84
PAPER & ENVELOPES 86
LAVISH LAMPSHADES 88
BOX FILES 90

RIT® DYE COLOR CHART 92
LIST OF SUPPLIERS 95

INTRODUCTION

I have always been excited by color, and in particular the way in which it changes the feel and mood of different materials. Color can affect the texture of a surface whether it be wood, card, paper or fabric.

I find it magical that a very ordinary, dull piece of cloth such as cotton or muslin can be transformed by the use of color. There are lots of projects in this book to inspire you – if a project is to your liking, but the range of colors isn't to your taste, then do it with a different color way.

I studied textiles at a college where the 'hands on' approach was encouraged, and I particularly loved messing about with dyes. So I was absolutely delighted when I was asked by my editor, Venetia Penfold, to write this book. My course was distinctly different from others of the time, with its strong emphasis on drawing and innovation, and experimentation with cloth and techniques. In those days it was a question of mixing dyes and chemicals with fixatives and binders. Now, companies such as *Rit* Dye have taken away all that hard work by producing wonderful ranges of colors and ancillary products to make our lives easy. Even as I write, new products and colors are being developed. So that you can keep up with these new developments, a list of suppliers and color charts are provided at the back of the book.

I hope that you have as much fun using the book and creating your own wonderful color combinations as I have had in writing it.

Juliet Bawden 1997

A BRIEF HISTORY OF DYEING

FOR THOUSANDS OF YEARS, COLORS FOR DYEING WERE OBTAINED FROM ANIMALS, VEGETABLES AND MINERALS. THE MIDDLE KINGDOM EGYPTIANS USED MADDER AND WELD AS DYES SO WELL THAT THEY ARE PRESERVED EVEN NOW. INDIGO WAS USED WIDELY IN JAPAN FROM AS FAR BACK AS THE SEVENTH CENTURY AND THE MEXICANS WERE DYEING WITH COCHINEAL LONG BEFORE THE SPANISH ARRIVED.

However, with the mechanization of the nineteenth century, spun and woven yarns were being produced in large quantities and very cheaply, and demand grew for better colors. Matching shades became important and 'fashion' colors were required. The dyeing process was beginning to struggle to keep up with the development of the yarn industry.

The turning point came with the discovery of synthetic dyes, the first by William Perkin, a student at the Royal College of Chemistry in London. He developed a way of producing a purple dye, and this discovery led to increased interest and research throughout Europe into ways of manufacturing synthetic dyes. In 1856, two chemists in Germany, Grabe and Lieberman, discovered a way to make alizarin. Alizarin is the compound found in the madder plant, which produces its red and brown coloring effects. From this came the discovery that synthetic dyes had durability and strength, and so followed the discovery of synthetic magenta, blues, violets, greens and reds.

Although these dyes produced brilliant colors on natural fibers, they were not colorfast, and so the fabrics would not hold the color. In 1868, this problem was approached with the solution of 'mordanting'. A mordant fixes color by encouraging an affinity between the dye and the fiber and so binds the dyestuffs to the fabric. Mordants can be found in natural dyes as well as being produced synthetically. Some natural dyes need a mordant and others do not. Mordants include iron, tin, salt, vinegar and caustic soda.

BATIK

Batik is a resist method of patterning cloth. Where a resist such as wax is applied, the cloth will remain its original color. During dyeing the dye seeps into any cracks or fissures in the wax, giving batik its characteristic look. A dyer can deliberately crack the wax more to create a marbled effect. Alternatively, the waxed cloth may be left in the sun to make the wax supple and less likely to crack. After dyeing, the resist is removed.

Some theories suggest that batik originated in China and then spread eastwards via Japan. Surprisingly, batik is a native craft of the Indian subcontinent. Traditionally, the southeast coast of India, from the Deccan plateau to Cape Comoran, was famous for its batik cloths. It is thought that batik was introduced into Java during the twelfth century by Indians who came to settle there and through trading links.

TIE DYE

Tie dye or 'Plangi' is a method of decorating cloth by isolating areas so that they resist the dye. The most popular way of doing this is to tie string or yarn around parts of the cloth. Other methods include folding, clipping, sewing and encircling small objects such as seeds.

Evidence of tie dye in India and Java dates from the sixth and seventh centuries. In western Liang, China, a piece of plangi from AD 418 has been found. In Japan, plangi patterned cloth was worn by all classes of society in the eleventh and twelfth centuries. Japanese tie dye was so intricate that it could take a year to tie the knots in a length of cloth and another year to undo them!

MATER

As you read *To Dye For* it will
the projects are very easy to do
way of special tools. Most of the
the kitchen table or with the help

TECHN

IALS &

become apparent that most of

and need little or nothing in the

techniques can be carried out on

of a domestic washing machine.

IQUES.

MATERIALS

NEARLY ALL THE REQUIRED MATERIALS CAN BE FOUND IN A CRAFT STORE, A FABRIC STORE OR AN ART-SUPPLY STORE. THIS CHAPTER LOOKS AT THE RANGE OF DYES AND EQUIPMENT CURRENTLY AVAILABLE.

TYPES OF DYES

Before starting, you need to find the correct dye for your material. No single dye will work on all fibers with the same effectiveness. In general, natural fabrics are most suitable for dyeing since they result in strong, clear colors, but that is not always the case. When choosing dyes always read the manufacturer's instructions, and always test a scrap of material before starting on the real piece. Dyes in different countries and those made by different manufacturers work in different ways, and the instructions will help you to get the best results from the product.

Acid Dyes

Acid dyes were discovered in 1875, and were developed from experimentation with the dye elements in natural dyestuffs and their production as a synthetic. They were found to work well with wool, silk and hairy fibers, in a water solution without the use of a mordant. To produce fast and bright colors, an acid dye has to be processed in acidic conditions, in a hot, acidulated dye bath, using vinegar instead of salt as a mordant.

Direct Dyes

These are simple to use, but have a low resistance to washing and therefore fade quickly. For this reason, this kind of dye is most suitable for fabrics that don't require frequent laundering (e.g. furnishings, such as drapes, rugs and hangings). They are ideal for rag rug dyeing.

Disperse Dyes

These were developed in 1923 to dye acetate rayon. This fiber could not be dyed by any existing methods, as dyes could not be dissolved in any substance that was compatible with rayon. These dyes disperse into water rather than dissolve, but they have to be used with a dispersing agent to keep the dye evenly distributed in the water, or the particles tend to sink to the bottom. They can be used on most synthetic fabrics: acetate, acrylic, nylon and polyester. Different variations need to be used depending on what fiber you will be dyeing.

Fiber Reactive Dyes

Developed to form stronger and more permanent bonds with fibers, these dyes are ideal for viscose, rayon, silk, linen, cotton and other plant fibers. The color range is not as wide as those for acid dyes, but the colors are brilliant and clear. Dyeing can be carried out in either hot or cold water, depending on the kind of reactive dye. Salt is used to encourage the dye molecules and the fibers to attract each other.

Mordant Dyes

These have no coloring property on their own, but when combined with metallic oxide will form color on cloth. The mordant has an affinity for both the cloth and the dyestuff.

Natural Dyes

These have been used since ancient times, but their use has declined with the progression of synthetic dyeing. However, there is a wealth of material available, and it is free. Experiment with leaves and stems, flower heads, roots, onion skins, berries and seeds. You can even use teabags.

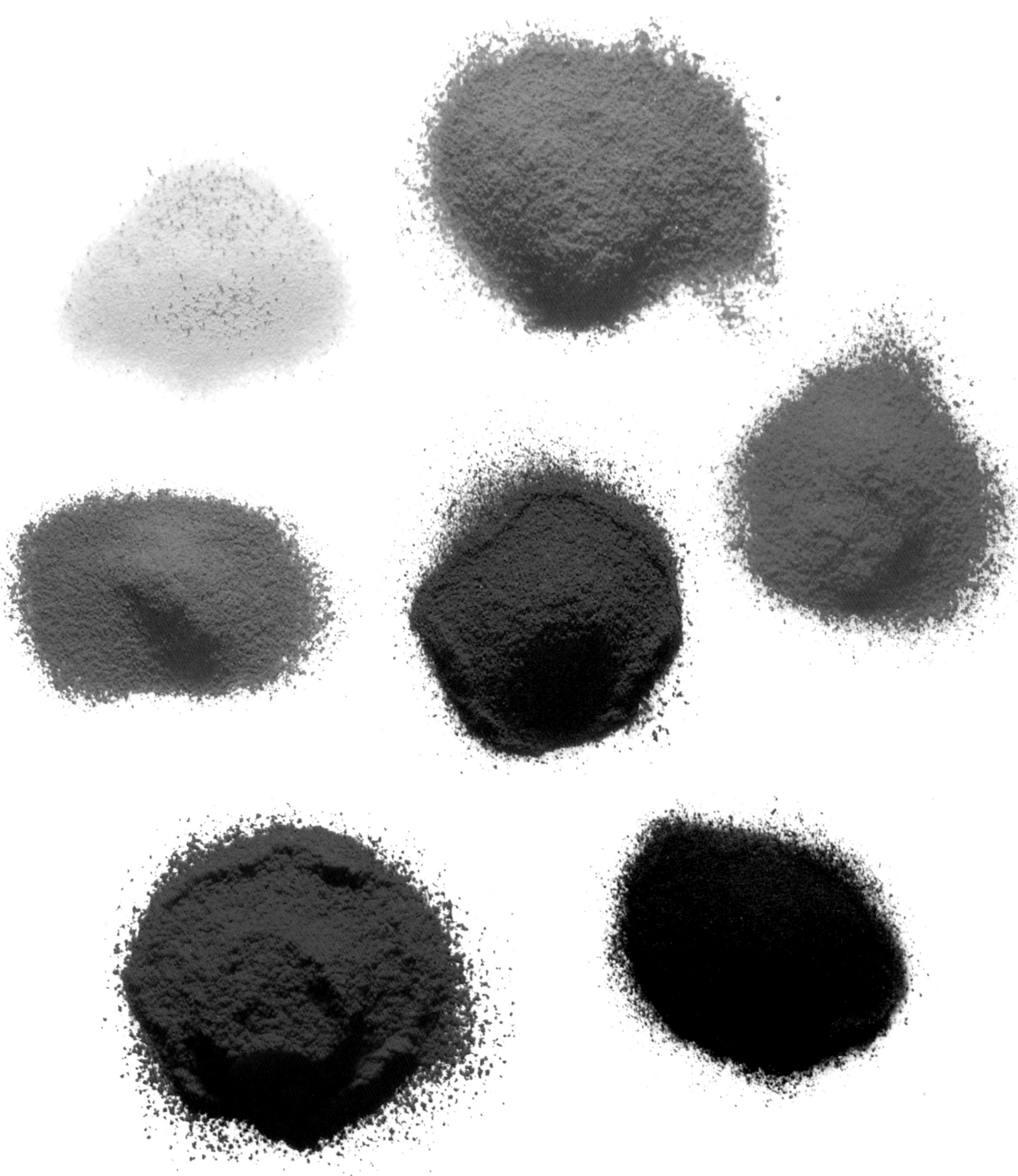

Synthetic Dyes

These are a mixture of finely ground chemicals which come in the form of powders, grains, granules or liquids. Different dye compounds are used for different purposes, although many of the dyes have similarities in the way they are used.

Commercial dye manufacturers make dyeing easy by selling small pots of dye which are mixed with a sachet of fixative and salt and then added to water. There are two main categories: cold water and hot water dyes. Cold water dyes are very stable and can withstand frequent washing, but are only suitable for natural fabrics. They are used mainly for tie dye and batik. Some, though not all, hot water dyes can be used in washing machines.

Equipment

Most of the equipment you need can be found in your kitchen, but always keep this equipment separate from cooking utensils, and ensure that dye implements are kept away from food at all times. Some equipment (e.g. string for tie dye) is specific to certain techniques and this is listed where appropriate.

Bottles

These are necessary to store stock solutions and chemicals. Old, screw-top food jars are ideal. Plastic is a safer and lighter alternative to glass, but will be stained by some dyes.

Dye Baths

A dye bath can be made from an old saucepan, canning pot, an old enamel bath or a clean bucket. Make sure the receptacle is large enough to agitate the cloth during dyeing.

Dye Pots

These should be heatproof and nonreactive. Glass, enamel and stainless steel are all suitable. Stainless steel is probably best as it is nonstaining, unbreakable and inert; a large old saucepan is ideal. It should be large enough to contain fiber or fabric at boiling temperatures, without boiling over.

Hairdryer

A useful tool for speeding up the drying process.

Heat Source

A gas or electric cooker is needed for heating, boiling and dyeing.

Iron and Ironing Board

Many dyes are fixed by ironing on the back. You will also need to iron the fabric when it has been dyed.

Measures and Weighing Implements

These will be needed to measure dye powders, stocks and fabrics. Graduated plastic beakers are good for measuring small amounts of dye stock. However, for more accurate measuring of smaller amounts measuring spoons are better — ¼ teaspoon, ½ teaspoon, 1 teaspoon and 1 tablespoon.
A 2 pint measuring jug is good for pouring solutions — make sure this is boil-proof, as the solutions will be very hot. Kitchen and/or bathroom scales are good for weighing fabrics.

Notebook

Essential for keeping a record of experiments, results and calculations for future reference.

Scissors

Essential when working with fabric. Keep one pair for fabric alone, as cutting paper with scissors blunts them.

Stirring Rods

Necessary for mixing solutions, stirring and manipulating hot, wet fabric and for transferring fabric from one place to another. Glass rods are good because they don't stain and are easy to clean. However, chopsticks or mixing spoons (wooden or plastic) will do the job just as well. Because wood will stain and perhaps transfer one color onto another, keep a collection of sticks to accommodate the colors you use.

Fabric

Many blends of over 50% synthetic yarns do not take dyes well, especially polyester. Some synthetics such as nylon and acetate dye very well with multi-purpose dyes. Most natural fabrics dye very well. Below are the most popular for home dyeing. Before dyeing fabric, it is advisable to test the material if possible. Experiment with a small piece of fabric (cut from a seam, hem or facing where it will not show) to determine the correct temperature and time required to achieve the color you desire. If you are unable to cut a sample from the article, use a piece of fabric of the same type and color.

Since dyed color appears slightly darker when wet, the fabric should be removed from the dye bath when it appears slightly darker than the color you actually want.

Most fabrics have a finish on them and this needs to be removed before they are dyed. The best way to do this is to wash the fabric in warm water with soap flakes. Some fabrics, such as cotton, may have to be boiled to lose their finish. Once the fabric has been washed it should be dried and ironed before beginning the dye process. The following list of fabrics can be used for home dyeing.

Cotton
This is a natural fiber. A great variety of finishing processes are applied to cottons and they can be blended with polyesters, wools, etc. Calico cotton is hardwearing and does not fray. Cambric cotton is soft to handle, presses fairly easily and will not fray. This slightly glossy cotton is suitable for gathering. Lawn cotton is a fine but crisp fabric and is ideal for most dyeing processes. It does not fray. Mercerized cotton has been treated with caustic soda to make it more receptive to dyestuffs. It is easy to handle, does not fray and is usually reversible. Gauze has a loose, uneven weave. It is inexpensive and good for block or stamp printing. Poplin is firm to handle and can be gathered and pressed.

Crêpe de Chine
These yarns are twisted before they are woven. The woven cloth is then wet finished to create a pebbly texture, and also to give it a slight stretch. The elasticity means that it drapes well.

Habutai and Pongee
These are tightly woven silks with plain weaves. Habutai used to mean that the silk was Japanese in origin — it now just refers to the silk being lightweight and plain woven. Pongee is a slightly heavier weight silk than Habutai.

Linen
This comes from the flax plant and is believed to have been the first textile fiber to have been used to weave cloth. It is more irregular in appearance than cotton, and can be dyed, printed and painted. However, it frays and creases badly.

Silk
This is obtained from the cocoon of the silk moth. It feels warm against the skin, drapes well, and is naturally crease resistant. It should always be washed before dyeing. Acid dyes work particularly well on silk, producing vibrant colors. Silk noil is made from the short fibers which surround the escape hole in a cocoon. It differs from other silks in that it is slightly off-white in color, and has nubbly flecks and a rough texture and muted color. It is not as durable as other silks and its slight background color will affect the end colors when hand painting.

Wool
This is a protein fiber. It can be spun, woven, felted and knitted. It is made into many kinds of cloth. The best for dyeing and hand painting are crêpes, jersey cloth and lightweight plain weaves.

TECHNIQUES

WHEN YOU ARE READY TO GET GOING, DO NOT BE AFRAID TO EXPERIMENT. TRY BATIK AND TIE DYE, SPONGING AND SPATTERING, AND, IF YOU HAVE NEVER TRIED IT, HAND PAINTING. YOU CAN CREATE ENDLESS DESIGNS ON FABRIC ONCE YOU BEGIN.

GETTING STARTED

When using dyestuffs and chemicals, safety is important. Always wear rubber gloves, an overall or apron, and a dust mask to keep from inhaling the dyes. (Some people are sensitive to dyes and can develop a rash on contact.) Covering your work surfaces with newspaper will make cleaning up easier. Work in a well-ventilated area and ensure that your equipment is clearly labeled. It must not be used for anything other than dyeing. Store dyes and chemicals in a clean, dry place and keep them out of the reach of children.

USING DIFFERENT DYES

Always refer to the manufacturer's instructions for the dye you intend to use and for the amount of dye and salt you will need for the weight of your fabric.

Multi-Purpose Dyes

These are ideal for dyeing small articles of clothing and fabric on the stove top or in the sink, and may also be used in the washing machine for larger articles such as bedspreads and curtains. They are also ideal for creating patterns, such as with batik and tie dye. Note that the guidelines outlined below apply to *Rit* Dyes.

The dyes are suitable for natural fabrics, synthetics, and blends where the majority of fiber is dyeable. They are not recommended for fabrics that are more than 50% polyester, fabrics that have rubber backing (such as bath mats or throw rugs), fabrics with special water-repellant finishes, and fabrics that are washable only in cold water or are labeled "Dry Clean Only". To care for dyed items, wash separately in cool water and mild detergent to minimize color fading.

Wash fabric first to remove finishes and stains. To achieve the color closest to that on the package, dye white or light-colored fabric. Use *Rit* Color Remover to remove stains or uneven color fading, and to lighten fabric color before dyeing to a lighter or completely different color. For best results when dyeing cotton, rayon, linen, ramie or blends of these fibers, add one cup of salt to the dye bath.

Prepare the dye solution by dissolving the dye powder thoroughly in hot water. Refer to the manufacturer's instructions for quantities. Always wear rubber gloves to protect the skin.

Instructions (Machine)

1. *Weigh and wash the fabric and leave damp.*
2. *Fill machine with enough hot water for fabric to move freely. Add predissolved dye; agitate to mix.*
3. *Add the fabric to the dye bath.*
4. *Set the machine for an extended wash cycle by resetting wash cycle before rinse cycle begins. (Fabric should be in dye bath for 30 minutes before rinsing begins.) Rinse in cold water until water runs clear. Wash deep shades in warm water and detergent.*
5. *Dry fabric in dryer or air dry.*
6. *Clean washing machine immediately with hot water, detergent, and one cup chlorine bleach using complete wash cycle. Wipe spills with chlorine bleach. Clean lint traps.*

Instructions (Stove Top)

(Recommended for black and other dark colors.)

1. *Weigh and wash the fabric and leave damp.*
2. *Fill pot with enough hot water for fabric to move freely. Add predissolved dye; stir to mix.*
3. *Add the fabric to the dye bath. Bring dye bath to simmer; stir constantly 30 to 60 minutes.*

4 *Rinse in warm water, then gradually cooler water until water runs clear. Wash fabric in warm water and detergent to remove remaining excess dye.*
5 *Dry item in dryer or air dry.*
6 *Clean pot immediately with chlorine bleach, then scrub with powdered cleanser if needed.*

Instructions (Sink or bucket)

(Recommended for dyeing small or delicate fabrics to a light or medium shade.)

1 *Weigh and wash the fabric and leave damp.*
2 *Fill sink or bucket with enough hot water for fabric to move freely. Add predissolved dye; stir to mix.*
3 *Add fabric to dye bath. Stir constantly 30 to 60 minutes.*
4 *Rinse in warm water, then gradually cooler water until water runs clear. For dark or deep shades of dye, wash fabric in warm water and detergent to remove excess dye.*
5 *Dry fabric in dryer or air dry.*
6 *Clean sink or bucket immediately with chlorine bleach, then scrub with powdered cleanser if needed.*

Cold Water Dyes

These are also good for use with batik and tie dye. Choose natural fabrics and avoid synthetics or fabrics with special finishes. Some manufacturers produce a fixative for cold water dyes which will make the fabric colorfast. (This is not necessary for wool — just use vinegar.)

For safety, remember that cold water dyes may produce an allergic reaction by inhalation or skin contact. Avoid breathing any dust from the dye.

Instructions

1 *Weigh, wash and rinse your fabric. For faded and streaky articles, you may be able to use a pre-dye color remover.*
2 *Fill a vessel with enough water to cover the fabric.*
3 *Wearing rubber gloves, dissolve the dye according to the manufacturer's instructions. Stir well, and add to the dye bath.*
4 *Dissolve salt and cold fixative in hottest tap water and add to the dye bath. If dyeing wool, add 11 fl oz vinegar instead of salt and fixative.*
5 *Put in clean, wet articles. Dye for 1 hour, agitating continually for the first 10 minutes, then occasionally for 50 minutes. Keep fabric submerged.*
6 *Rinse articles in cold water until the water runs clear. Then wash separately in hot water and washing detergent. Use lukewarm water for wool and silk.*
7 *Dry garment or cloth away from direct sunlight.*

Handy Hints

- The most successful dyeing is done on white or natural colored fabrics.
- You cannot successfully dye a light color on top of a darker one, although you can dye to change a color if the original is not too dark. For example, a yellow piece of cloth dyed blue will result in a shade of green.
- With some brands of dye you can remove some of the original color to make a lighter background color.
- The longer the fabric is in the dye bath with a hot water dye, the deeper the resulting color.
- Printed fabrics, or those with some white in their background, can be dyed very successfully. (See the polka dot hat boxes on page 56 and gingham pillows on page 66.)
- Dyes can be used to stain wood. Remember to remove any paint or varnish beforehand or the dye will be resisted. And bear in mind that the wood's color and grain will affect the resulting depth of color. Soft, light-colored woods such as pine will dye more easily and with fewer coats than hardwoods such as oak or cherry.
- Dyes can be used successfully on card and paper in both pale and deep tones.

Creating Patterns

While you can use dye just to transform the existing qualties and color of a fabric, the different dyeing techniques available also allow you to achieve an enormous range of decorative effects. Outlined below are a variety of ways to achieve patterns.

Basic Batik

The most suitable fabric for batik is fine natural fabric, as it is most absorbent of hot wax and cold dyes. Silk, cotton, linen and gauze are all ideal. For a large project, choose a 100% cotton sheet.

Materials

Dye Use a multi-purpose, cold water or a reactive dye to prevent dye from bleeding when the wax is boiled off. The fixative (only necessary for cold water dyes) and the dye should be kept separate until needed and then mixed together just before submerging the fabric. Once mixed, the fixative only remains stable for 2 hours.

Frame You need an adjustable wooden slot frame. It is made of four lengths of wood with slots cut at regular intervals along one long side of each piece, allowing the frame to be fitted together to make different sizes of frame. Alternatively, use canvas stretchers, an old picture frame, or even just tape the material to a table covered with a protective surface, as the wax will go through the fabric.

Metal pot The best way to heat wax is in a specially designed melting pot. If you don't have one of these, place the wax in a discarded food can in a saucepan of water kept on a low heat. Keep an eye on the water level and replenish it if it drops too low (it should be half way up the can).

Thermometer This is necessary to check the wax is at a constant temperature of 190°F.

Tjanting This wooden-handled tool has a metal wax container with a spout for drawing with wax. Brushes and cotton safety swabs may also be used for drawing hot wax onto stretched fabric. Once used for this purpose a brush will no longer be of use for anything else, so keep it as a batik brush.

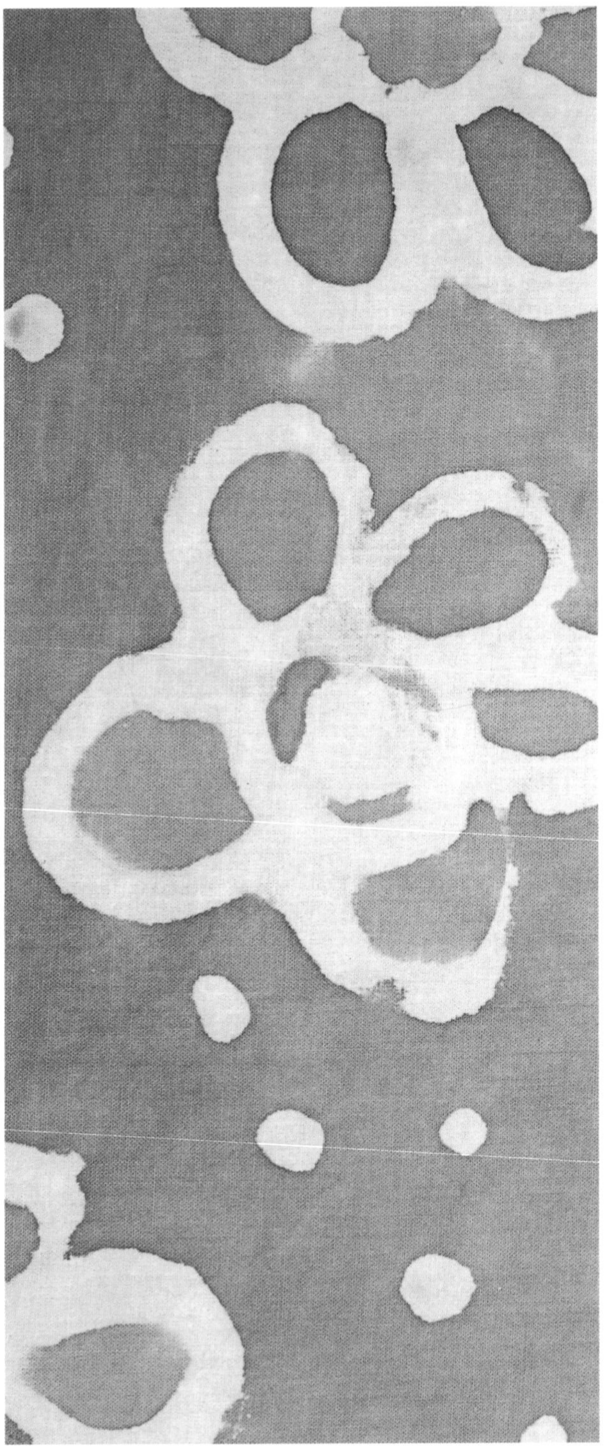

Batik fabric with flower and dot design

Tjap A metal printing block which is dipped into hot wax and stamped out onto fabric. Make your own by sticking old metal waste onto a block of wood.

Wax Candles can be melted down and used with beeswax. (Beeswax cannot be used by itself as it is too soft to give a good crackle.) Candles and paraffin wax can both be bought in hardware shops. Batik wax can be bought from craft shops, and comes in split-pea sized pieces which melt quickly.

Instructions

1 *Trace a design onto the fabric and stretch this tightly over a frame.*
2 *Fill the tjanting with molten wax and begin to draw it across the fabric.*
3 *If you are dyeing more than one color, paint over all the areas you wish to be the background color, say white, with the wax.*
4 *Allow the wax to dry, then dip the fabric into the lightest color dye (e.g. yellow).*
5 *When the cloth is dyed, you apply more wax to the areas you wish to remain yellow. You have now preserved the background white and yellow.*
6 *Dye the cloth again, say in blue, and so on. The cloth has more wax applied as the design builds up.*
7 *The final dye bath is the deepest.*
8 *The wax can be removed once the cloth is dry from the last dye bath. This can be done by scraping it off with a palette knife and then ironing it between sheets of unprinted paper. It can also be boiled off in water. Remember, never put waxy water down the sink or it will block it. You can actually re-use old wax if you collect it from the water when it cools.*

Hand Painting

This is a most versatile technique, allowing you to experiment with freehand and decorative painting. It can be carried out using any number of products and tools for painting. As well as standard paintbrushes, a variety of materials may be used to create textured backgrounds, including feathers, combs, sponges, and woven and knitted fabrics. Note that it is almost impossible to get a flat spread of color using dye on its own.

Instructions

1 *Mix the dye with the salt and fixative according to the manufacturer's instructions.*
2 *You will usually need to paint onto a heavy-duty fabric, such as canvas. Place the fabric on a table and secure the corners with masking tape.*
3 *If you want to transfer a particular design to fabric, you can draw the pattern out first in pencil.*
4 *Apply a little dye at a time. Brush it on to get an almost crayon-like effect.*
5 *If you require more density of color, the dyes may begin to bleed a little into one another, so allow for this in the original design.*

Canvas painted with dark-blue dye

Color Gradation

The technique of color gradation offers a rich and subtle shift of color between two hues (see the gauze curtains on page 34).

Materials

Multi-purpose or cold water dyes: 3 colors
Gauze or fine lawn
Large bowl
Fixative (for cold water dye only)
Salt
Plastic wrap

Instructions

1. *Wash the fabric and squeeze out the excess water.*
2. *Mix the lightest color with the salt and fixative (only necessary for cold water dyes) in a large bowl and place it in the sink. Immerse all the fabric for the correct amount of time (see manufacturer's instructions for cold water dyes).*
3. *Empty the first color. Squeeze out excess dye and cover the first third of the fabric in plastic wrap. Put to one side.*
4. *Mix up the second color as before. Immerse the two-thirds of fabric which are not wrapped in plastic wrap and leave as before.*
5. *Leaving the first piece of plastic wrap, cover half the remaining dyed piece in plastic wrap. Mix up the third dye bath as before.*
6. *Add the last third of unwrapped fabric to this dye bath.*
7. *Once dyeing is complete, unwrap the plastic and rinse the fabric.*
8. *Wash in warm soapy water and then leave to dry.*

Color gradation

Sponging and Spattering

Neither of these techniques have a history, although both were widely used in the 1980s as decorative finishes for interiors. They can be used with cold water or multi-purpose dyes to great effect – without any drawing skills. The random results can be controlled to a certain extent.

Instructions (sponging)

1. *Sponging is best applied with a natural sea sponge, although ordinary household sponges may also be used.*
2. *Before applying the cold water or multi-purpose dye to the cloth, dab any excess onto a spare piece of fabric or paper. This gives a much clearer design, showing the pores and undulations of the sponge on the material.*
3. *Apply the dye with a dryish sponge which is dabbed onto the cloth. It is best to start with the palest color, and work through to the darkest color.*

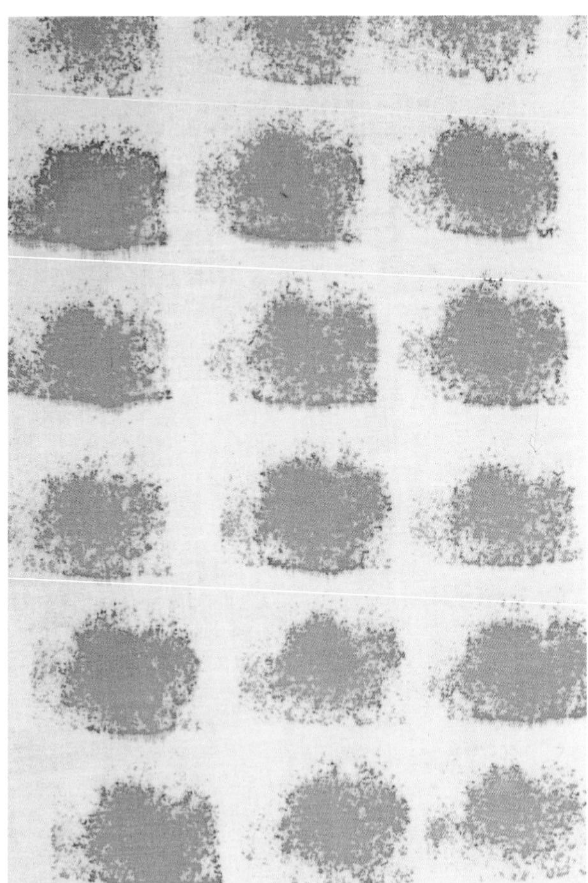

A rectangular piece of sponge created this regular pattern

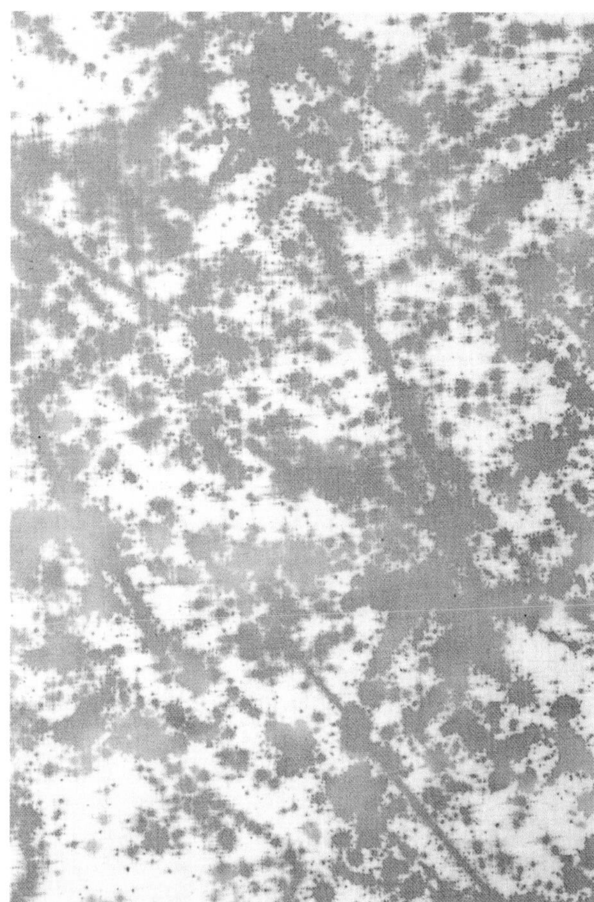

Spattering effect with a paintbrush loaded with blue dye

Instructions (spattering)

1. *Use a limited palette of one or two colors on a different colored background.*
2. *Before starting a project, practice on some sample fabric.*
3. *As spattering is messy, cover everything in newspaper, wear old clothes and, if possible, work outside.*
4. *You can vary the finished results by the size of the brush, the amount of dye on the brush and your own strength when flicking the paint.*
5. *Try rubbing a finger along the bristles of a paint-loaded toothbrush to produce a much finer array of color spots than you can get with a large artist's paintbrush. The latter will usually produce a line or arc of color, finished with a blob of paint.*
6. *This method of decorating cloth takes a long time to dry, but you can speed it up with a hairdryer.*

Stamping

Stamping enables you to create your own random or regular design on fabric. You can use the same stamp and vary the color of the dye, or combine different shaped stamps.

Materials

Cotton fabric
Multi-purpose or cold water dye: blue
Rubber gloves
Fixative
Salt
Rubber stamp
Saucer
Masking tape
Paintbrush

Instructions

1. *Mix the dye with the salt and fixative (only necessary for cold water dyes) according to the instructions.*
2. *Place the fabric on a table and secure the corners with masking tape.*
3. *Paint the dye on the stamp. As dye is liquid, you will only need a small amount.*
4. *Hold the stamp vertically and press it onto the fabric. Repeat until the fabric is covered with the design.*

Fabric stamped with a star motif

Tie Dye

The best fabrics for tie dye are the finer ones which can be tied more tightly and therefore make more intricate patterns and motifs. Cotton, silk, wool or synthetics are all suitable. The different tie-dye shapes are outlined below:

Circles Tie round objects such as stones, seeds, beans, marbles or buttons into the fabric. Or the fabric can just be drawn up into a peak and bound with thread.

Stripes The fabric is pleated or rolled and then bound at regular intervals. (Lengthwise for vertical stripes, widthwise for horizontal stripes, and diagonally for diagonal stripes.) It is best to iron the pleats for really crisp lines.

Motifs (figures or animals) Tie tiny seeds or stones in the figure's shape. When dyed and undone, the shape appears as a dotted drawing.

Chevron pattern Pleat the material like an accordian, iron to flatten the pleats, and then arrange the bulldog clips so that they form a zig-zag along each edge of the pleated cloth. In the same way, use clothespins to create slightly irregular, square shapes on the fabric.

Marbling Tie the fabric in a ball and bind it very tightly in a random way.

Random pattern Place paper clips around the edge of a folded piece of cloth to create another interesting pattern.

Materials

Multi-purpose or hand dye
Fine cotton fabric
Rice
Thread
Non-metallic container
Plastic wrap
Microwave oven
Rubber gloves
Washing powder

Instructions (microwave method)

1. *Tie the fabric by encircling grains of rice and tying with thread.*
2. *Wet the fabric.*
3. *Wearing rubber gloves and a face mask, open the dye and put in the non-metallic container. (For safety it is important not to use metal in a microwave.)*
4. *Add ½ pint warm tap water and stir.*
5. *Add ½ pint cold water.*
6. *Submerge the tied cloth in the dye mixture.*
7. *Cover with plastic wrap and place in the microwave for 4 minutes on high.*
8. *Remove the fabric from the bowl and then rinse it under running water until the water runs clear.*
9. *Wash in hot water with washing powder and leave to dry.*
10. *Remove the knots. The cloth will now be fixed with its tie dye pattern.*

Instructions (traditional method)

1. *Tie, fold, clip and pin the fabric as above.*
2. *Mix the dye with the salt and fixative (only necessary for cold water dyes) according to the manufacturer's instructions and place in the dye bath.*
3. *Place the tied pieces in the dye bath and leave for the correct amount of time (see manufacturer's instructions).*
4. *Take the pieces of fabric out of the dye bath and leave to dry before removing the tied items.*
5. *Once dry, remove the string, ties etc., and iron the pieces of fabric flat.*

Top left: *folded and clothespinned fabric*
Top right: *clothespinned fabric*
Bottom left: *fabric tie dyed with beans*
Bottom right: *marbled fabric*

Color

I cannot write a book on dyeing without referring to its essence — Color.

Color surrounds us everywhere we look and in everything we touch. It stimulates our senses, affecting moods and attitudes without our knowledge. When one color is placed beside another, the combination can lead to differing perceptions of those colors. Even the circumstances in which colors are seen affect our perception, as various colors give different experiences.

Color Associations

One color can have a vast range of different shades and hues. Certain colors are known to have specific psychological effects — blue is tranquil, yellow is energizing, green is soothing and red is stimulating. Colors also have associations for many people according to their geographical location and culture.

Yellow is a holy color in Southeast Asia. It is symbolic of purity and dedication in Buddhist communities (hence the color of robes worn by Buddhist monks). It is happy, childlike and cheerful, having natural associations with the sun. Many people like to decorate cold and uninviting rooms in yellows.

Orange is yellow's nearest relation, another soft, bright, warm color, reminiscent of early sunsets and glowing fires.

Green, too, is a holy color, this time for Muslims. Perceived as calm and reverent, it is linked with nature. It is also a color which in many cultures represents the natural cycle of life and death. It has for centuries signified good luck, as well as envy, greed and jealousy. It is an 'anchoring color', holding together the bright colors of flowers and berries. Hence it is a good background for a vivid color scheme.

Blue is another color with numerous natural associations. It has an almost infinite quality, depending on its numerous shades. It is refreshing, serene, restful and expansive. Blue can be visualized in hues from the violet-blue of wildflowers, bluebells, hyacinths, and the turquoise-blue of the ocean, to the deep navy-blue of the midnight sky and the azure sky of a hot summer's day. Think also of the jewel hues of sapphires, lapis lazuli, and aquamarines. Often seen as a cold color, its shades and hues actually cover a range of moods. Blue outsells all other colors for clothing and interiors.

Red is a hot and passionate color. The dominant force in a color scheme, it demands attention. It is the color of blood, deadly yet life-enforcing. In Asia, red is the traditional choice for weddings. In China, New Year celebrations are dominated by red, which signifies good luck and happiness. The color of ripe sweet fruit and tempting poisonous berries, it is also the color of that timeless love token, the red rose. It also has wrathful connotations, signalling danger. Because of the difficulty in stabilizing red as a dye, it was little used in the past and has only been harnessed with modern technology.

Color on Textiles

The elements which infuse a home with personality and warmth are the accessories and colors, usually the surrounding textiles: upholstery, pillows, curtains, carpets and rugs. No matter what the texture of the fabrics, they will always soften the surroundings, because the nature of fabric is generally tactile.

Working with color on textiles differs greatly from working with color on other mediums. Explore how fibers and colors affect one another when they are placed side-by-side. You can then use the juxtapositions of a rough texture against a smooth and a dull texture against a shiny one. You will see that colors vary greatly when placed together; they are never predictable or constant and will often be very unlike your expectations.

Fabrics and fibers accept dyes differently, giving different tones and shades according to the coarseness or smoothness of the fiber. The smooth surfaces of silk and nylon reflect light, giving the fabric a luster and brightness. However, cotton, wool and flax, which are either hairy or have been flattened, have irregular surfaces, so that they absorb more light than smooth fabrics and appear dull and dark.

If you lay a piece of silk alongside a piece of wool dyed the same color, the silk appears brighter because it has a smoother quality. Remember that you cannot always predict how a color will turn out; when a piece of raffia was dyed in turquoise, for example, it gave a bright grass green color! With this in mind it is helpful to have a warm iron handy, so that while dyeing you can match colors. Do this by removing a piece of fabric from the dye bath and cutting off a sample which may be rinsed in cool water and pressed dry. In this way you can determine how the color will appear when dry.

Dyes are the  ideal medium for revamping a tired

including pillows, curtains and rugs. They can be used to decorate the

there are instructions for dyeing canvas  purple and

S P A

ING

environment.  They are great on small accessories,

mundane object to make it extra special. For example,

pomegranate to replace old or dull director's chair seats.

PATCHWORK THROW

A MODERN VERSION OF TIE DYE, TAKING AWAY THAT SIXTIES' HIPPIE IMAGE. INDIVIDUALLY DYED PIECES OF FABRIC SEWN ONTO AN INDIGO BACKING GIVE A LOOK OF JAPANESE MINIMALISM.

MATERIALS

Multi-purpose dye: blue
Fine white cotton lawn
Cotton lawn for backing
Fusible webbing
Dye bath
Salt
Rubber gloves
Iron
Sewing materials
(scissors, pins, matching thread and needles)
Clothespins, coins, rice, paper clips, string

INSTRUCTIONS

1. Cut the lawn into 9 in squares, and tie, fold, clip and clothespin each piece to form your own design. (Refer to the tie dye instructions on page 22.)
2. Mix the dye, salt and fixative according to the manufacturer's instructions. Place in the dye bath.
3. Place the tied pieces and the backing piece in the dye bath and leave for the correct amount of time (see manufacturer's instructions).
4. Take the pieces out and leave to dry before removing the ties and the objects you have used.
5. Iron the squares.
6. Iron fusible webbing onto the back of each square.
7. Cut the pieces into smaller squares to the size you desire.
8. Arrange these squares on the backing fabric. Leave a border space between each shape.
9. Pull off the paper backing and iron each square into place.
10. Using a zig-zag stitch, sew around each piece of tie dye. Finally, turn under the edges of the backing fabric, pin, and sew to neaten the edges.

Finished size: 49 x 60 in

VELVET PILLOWS

WHITE COTTON VELVET DYES BEAUTIFULLY, GIVING A WONDERFUL RICHNESS IN COLOR AND TEXTURE. WE USED REDS, HOT ORANGE, YELLOW, PURPLE AND DEEP BLUES.

MATERIALS

Multi-purpose dyes: purple, yellow, orange and blue
100% cotton velvet
Pillow forms
Salt
Rubber gloves
Iron
Sewing machine and thread
Sewing materials
Tassels and trims

INSTRUCTIONS

Note: Make sure you have enough velvet to make an envelope-backed pillow cover.

1. Wet the velvet and then follow the manufacturer's instructions for machine dyeing (see page 16).
2. Take out the fabric and leave to dry.
3. Iron the reverse side of the fabric and cut a pillow front ⅜ in larger all the way around than the pillow form.
4. Cut two pieces for the back of the pillow which are each the same width as the pillow front but only two-thirds of its length. These will overlap one another so that when the pillow is inserted, it will be covered.
5. To prepare the back, machine stitch a hem 1 in along the side of each piece of fabric. These hems will eventually overlap.
6. Tack or baste the two back pieces so that the hemmed edges overlap by 4 in. When basted they should be the same size as the pillow front.
7. Pin the front and back together with right sides facing, then machine sew, allowing a ⅜ in seam.
8. Sew tassels onto the corners of some pillows and braiding around the edges of others.

Finished size: 16 sq in

DIRECTOR'S CHAIR

DIRECTORS' CHAIRS ARE A STYLISH AND PRACTICAL WAY OF PROVIDING EXTRA SEATING. BY DYEING YOUR OWN FABRIC YOU CAN CREATE AN ORIGINAL COLOR SCHEME.

MATERIALS

Multi-purpose dyes: orange, purple
Strong fabric (e.g. canvas)
Director's chair
3M Fabric Finish
Salt
Rubber gloves
Iron
Sewing materials
Tracing paper for pattern

INSTRUCTIONS

1 Remove the existing fabric from the director's chair and use this as a template to cut a pattern for the new fabric.

2 Cut enough fabric to make a new chair cover. (Note that you are not cutting the pattern at this stage.) Make sure that there is enough fabric for seam allowances and for shrinkage when dyeing, as this often occurs with natural fabrics.

3 Dye the fabric according to the manufacturer's instructions (see page 16).

4 Leave the fabric to dry.

5 Iron flat, and then, using the pattern you made in step one, cut a new seat cover and backing. Sew the cover together, taking care to use several rows of stitching as the seat will have to support someone. Place on the chair and adjust to fit if necessary.

6 Treat the canvas seat with fabric finish in order to resist stains and prevent dye rubbing off onto clothing.

Finished size: Back 27 x 8 in
Seat 28½ x 16½ in

GAUZE CURTAINS

THESE RED-HOT AND VIBRANT GAUZE CURTAINS USE THE EFFECTIVE DYEING METHOD OF COLOR GRADATION. A STRIKING COMBINATION OF RED, PINK AND ORANGE DYES WERE USED.

MATERIALS

Multi-purpose or cold water dyes: orange, pink and red
Gauze
Large bowl
Fixative (for cold water dyes only)
Salt
Rubber gloves
Sink with draining board
Plastic wrap

INSTRUCTIONS

Note: As gauze is rather narrow and very fine it may be better to dye two or three lengths of cloth together, and then cut the curtain to fit your window.

1 Wash the fabric and squeeze out excess water (see instructions on page 20).

2 Mix the lightest color dye with the salt and fixative (only necessary for cold water dyes) in the bowl and put this in the sink. Follow the manufacturer's instructions (see pages 16 and 17) and place the fabric in the bowl for as long as is needed for the dye to take.

3 Empty the first color out of the bowl and down the sink. Squeeze out the excess dye and cover the first third of the fabric in plastic wrap.

4 Put the first plastic-wrapped piece of fabric on the draining board. Mix up the second color, adding salt and fixative. Add the unwrapped fabric to this dye bath and leave as you did the first color.

5 Leaving the first piece of plastic wrap in place, wrap half of the next piece of dyed fabric in plastic wrap. Mix up the third, and darkest, dye bath.

6 Add the last piece of unwrapped fabric to the dye bath.

7 When all the fabric has been dyed, unwrap and rinse the fabric. Leave it to dry.

8 Turn the hems under and under again, and sew with either a running or hemming stitch.

Finished size: 25 ft x 39 in

SOFA THROW

THIS SOFA THROW IS MADE FROM WOOLS DYED IN STRIPS AND THEN SEWN TOGETHER. IT IS INSPIRED BY THE COLORS OF HEATHER, INCLUDING BLUE, LILAC, CHARCOAL GRAY, AND SOFT GREEN.

MATERIALS

Multi-purpose dyes: purple, green and blue
2¼ yd length woolen fabric
Salt
Rubber gloves
Sewing machine

INSTRUCTIONS

1 Cut the fabric into strips 2¼ ft x 8 in. If you are dyeing in a washing machine there will be some shrinkage, and the colors will be softer.

2 Dye the fabric according to the manufacturer's instructions (see page 16). Leave to dry.

3 Place the pieces next to one another and arrange until you have a pleasing composition.

4 Using a zig-zag stitich, abut the pieces of fabric, pin, and then machine together to build up a blanket of stripes.

5 Go back and forth up each row with the zig-zag stitch to make a strong seam. Finally, sew around the edge of the throw with a zig-zag stitch to give a neat finish.

DAISIES UNDERFOOT

THIS PRETTY LITTLE MAT IS MADE FROM CANVAS WITH A DAISY DESIGN DRAWN ON IT IN PENCIL AND THEN FILLED IN WITH PASTEL DYES.

MATERIALS

Multi-purpose or cold water dyes: pale blue and pale yellow
2 pieces of artist's canvas 34 x 20 in
Glass jars
Paintbrush
Blue crayon
Rubber gloves
Iron
Ruler
Pencil
Sewing materials
Tracing paper
Thin card

INSTRUCTIONS

1 Take one piece of canvas and mark out eight evenly spaced rectangles, four at the top and four at the bottom.

2 Draw a simple daisy shape. Trace this image on to card and cut it out to make a template.

3 Draw around the template onto each of the rectangles. Complete the center of the design in freehand.

4 Mix the dyes in the glass jars according to the manufacturer's instructions (see pages 16 and 17). Paint in the backgrounds and daisies as shown in the photograph.

5 Go over the lines with a soft blue crayon to give definition. Iron the fabric on the back to fix the design.

6 Allowing a ⅜ in seam, turn in the raw edges and pin the decorated front onto the back. Sew the two pieces together.

CHEST OF DRAWERS

AS YOU WILL SEE FROM THIS CHEST OF LIGHTWOOD DRAWERS, WOOD ACCEPTS COLOR BEAUTIFULLY. A SOFT PALETTE OF BLUES, GREENS AND MAUVES WAS USED.

MATERIALS

Multi-purpose or cold water dyes: blues, greens and mauves
Softwood chest of drawers
Wooden handles (optional)
Glass jars
Fine sandpaper
Sponge
Rubber gloves
Clear polyurethane varnish (optional)
Paintbrush

INSTRUCTIONS

1. Sand each drawer and brush off any loose particles.
2. Dissolve each dye in water according to the manufacturer's instructions (see pages 16 and 17).
3. Apply the dissolved dye with a sponge, sponging in the direction of the grain. Put each drawer to one side and leave to dry before working on the next drawer.
4. Allow to dry thoroughly before applying the next coat. The more colors you add, the deeper the finished color. Remember that the drawers will look darker when wet than once they are dry.
5. If using wooden handles, drop them in the dye pots and agitate occasionally to get even coverage. When the color is dense enough, remove and leave to dry.
6. Screw the handles into the drawers. Give each drawer a coat of varnish if you wish to seal it.

TAB CURTAINS

THESE HEAVY DUTY CANVAS CURTAINS WERE DYED BRIGHT YELLOW IN A WASHING MACHINE. TO GET EVEN COVERAGE, FOLLOW THE DYEING INSTRUCTIONS TO THE LETTER.

MATERIALS

Multi-purpose dye: yellow
Canvas
Lining fabric
Salt
Rubber gloves
Iron-on interfacing
(for tie backs and valances)
Iron and ironing board
Sewing materials
Tracing paper
Pencil

INSTRUCTIONS

1. The canvas and lining fabric should measure the width by the length of each curtain, plus a 12 in seam allowance, plus enough fabric for the tabs, placed every 4 in.
2. Wash, dry and then machine dye the fabric according to the manufacturer's instructions (see page 16).
3. To make the curtain tabs, double the measurement from the top of the curtain rail to the top of the window. Draw a pattern on tracing paper using a 2 in width.
4. Transfer the pattern onto the interfacing and cut out the tabs.
5. Cut the fabric ⅜ in larger all the way around than the pattern. Iron the interfacing tab into the center of the wrong side of the fabric. Turn the edges in and iron into position. You may have to cut away excess fabric at this point.
6. Cut the lining fabric for your tabs, slightly smaller than the outer fabric. Press under the seam allowance and sew the lining onto the back of the tab so the raw edges and interfacing are hidden.
7. Now cut the canvas and lining fabric for your curtains. The lining is 4 in narrower than the outer curtain on either side. With right sides facing, join the lining to the outer curtain down the two long sides. Turn right sides out and iron so that the lining is 3½ in from the side on either side of the curtain back.
8. Turn the top of the curtain and the lining in towards the center and pin the tabs at even intervals so they are sandwiched between the curtain front and back. Sew into position using a running stitch.
9. Adjust the curtains to fit the pole. Pin the hem and leave to hang for a few days before hemming.

EMBROIDERED PILLOWS

EMBROIDERED PILLOWS WITH WHITE WORKED ON WHITE OR PILLOWS MADE WITH LACE CAN START TO LOOK TIRED. WITH DYEING, YOU CAN GIVE THEM A NEW LEASE ON LIFE AND GIVE A ROOM INTERESTING COLORED ACCENTS.

MATERIALS

Multi-purpose dyes: blues
White embroidered pillows
and/or white lace or embroidery
Cotton fabric
Dye bath
Salt
Rubber gloves
Iron

INSTRUCTIONS

1 Wash the pillow covers.

2 Dye according to the manufacturer's instructions for machine dyeing (see page 16).

3 Iron flat.

4 Fit pillow pads back in pillow covers.

Alternative ideas

Make your own dyed pillow covers using old lace and new cotton fabric dyed together. Sew the lace on top of the cotton and make the pillow cover as for the velvet pillows on page 30.

BEDRO

Dyeing can come into its own in the bedroom, most obviously for sheets and pillowcases. Terry towels and robes can also be dyed, and this is a very good way to invigorate tired, once white, bedroom accessories. Dyed furniture, rugs and hat boxes all make gay additions to a bedroom.

OMS

DUVET COVER & PILLOWCASES

WHAT COULD BE NICER THAN DYEING YOUR OWN BED LINEN? IT IS BEST TO USE 100% COTTON LINENS, WHICH CAN BE BOUGHT OR MADE. WE USED MAUVE AND LIGHT-BLUE MULTI-PURPOSE DYES.

MATERIALS

Multi-purpose dyes: blues and mauves
Cotton pillowcases
100% cotton fabric
9½ x 7½ ft
Salt
Rubber gloves
Iron
Sewing materials
Snap tape

INSTRUCTIONS

1. Dye one half of the fabric and a pillowcase in one of your chosen colors in the washing machine, and the other half of the fabric and a second pillowcase the second color (see instructions on page 16).
2. Leave to dry and iron flat.
3. Take the blue sheet and turn under one narrow side by ¼ in and then again by ¼ in. Sew with a running stitch. Repeat this process on the lilac sheeting.
4. With right sides together and the two hemmed edges facing one another, sew the lilac to the blue on three sides, leaving the hemmed side as the opening.
5. Close the remaining gap by sewing on a strip of snaps on a tape, or make ties from any excess fabric.

Finished size: Measure your duvet and add ⅜ in seam allowance all the way around and cut the front and back to this dimension.

TERRIFIC TOWELS

THERE IS AN AMAZING COLOR RANGE OF DYES ON THE MARKET – EVEN WIDER THAN THAT AVAILABLE FOR TOWELS. DYEING ALLOWS YOU TO CREATE A COLLECTION OF TOWELS TO COMPLEMENT YOUR ROOM. MAKE SURE YOU CHOOSE GOOD QUALITY TOWELS.

MATERIALS

Multi-purpose dyes: purple, orange, yellow and pink
White towels
Salt
Rubber gloves

INSTRUCTIONS

1. Wet the towels and follow the manufacturer's instructions for machine dyeing (see page 16).
2. Leave to dry and then put in a tumble dryer to puff up the pile, which may have flattened during the dyeing process.

Alternative ideas

Buy terry cloth fabric and make your own towels and dye them. You can also dye terry cloth bathrobes and face-cloths. You can dye colored towels but they will need to be dyed darker than the original color.

DOTTY HAT BOXES

YOU CAN DYE POLKA DOT FABRICS TO GREAT EFFECT. DEPENDING ON THE STRENGTH OF COLOR IN THE FABRIC AND THE DYE, YOU CAN TRANSFORM THE COLORS IN A FABRIC OR COLOR THE LIGHTER AREAS.

MATERIALS

Polka dot fabric in 100% cotton
(small box 1¼ x 2 yds
medium box 1¼ x 2 yds
large box 1¼ x 2⅞ yds)
Cardboard hat boxes
Multi-purpose dyes: turquoise, pink, blue and brown
Salt
Rubber gloves
Iron
Batting
Glue
Scissors
Ruler

INSTRUCTIONS

1. Follow the manufacturer's instructions for machine dyeing (see page 16).
2. Once the fabric is dry and ironed flat, cut one circle the diameter of the lid plus another the size of the base, adding ⅜ in for turnings to each.
3. Cut a piece of batting exactly the size of the lid.
4. Cut one oblong of fabric the size of the box side and another the size of the lid rim. Allow a 1 in turning on each.
5. Cut ⅜ in deep snips around the edge of the base fabric. Turn the box upside-down and cover the base with glue. Center the fabric over the base and smooth out from the center. Glue down the snipped edges.
6. Press a ⅜ in turning along the wrong side of one long edge of the box side fabric. Attach fabric so pressed edge is level with box base. Turn the box as you glue and fold the overlapping end under.
7. Glue a ⅝ in seam allowance to the inside edge, snipping the fabric as needed to make it smooth and flat.
8. Cover the box lid as you have the side, but first glue the batting in place.

Finished size: small box 10 in
medium box 11½ in
large box 17 in

RUSTIC STOOL

THIS SMALL RUSTIC STOOL HAS A TRADITIONAL AND QUITE CHARMING DESIGN. IT IS MADE FROM A SOFT WOOD AND PAINTED USING TWO NON-TRADITIONAL COLORED DYES.

MATERIALS

Multi-purpose or cold water dyes: blue and red
Soft wood stool
Glass jars
Sponge
Fine paintbrush
Sandpaper
Rubber gloves
Clear polyurethane varnish (optional)

INSTRUCTIONS

1. Sand the stool, taking care to get into all the corners and places where the legs join onto the top. Brush away all dust.
2. Mix the dyes according to the manufacturer's instructions (see pages 16 and 17).
3. With a sponge, apply the first dye to the top of the stool. Use a paintbrush to touch up any inaccessible corners. Leave to dry completely.
4. Turn upside-down and paint the dye on the underside of the stool seat. Leave to dry.
5. Apply the contrasting color dye to the legs. Use a paintbrush in the areas where the legs join onto the stool seat.
6. If the color is not deep enough, go over each section of the stool with another coat of dye, remembering to leave it to dry before going on to the next section.
7. Apply a coat of polyurethane varnish if you wish to seal the dye.

TRUE BLUE PILLOWS

DENIM, DRILL AND CHAMBRAY FOR SOFT FURNISHINGS LOOK GOOD ON THEIR OWN OR TOGETHER. A VARIETY OF TOUGH COTTON AND LINEN FABRICS WERE DYED IN DIFFERENT SHADES OF DENIM.

MATERIALS

Multi-purpose dyes: blues
100% cotton fabrics
Pillow forms
Salt
Rubber gloves
Iron
Sewing materials
Cotton piping or braid

INSTRUCTIONS

Note: You will need enough fabric to make an envelope-backed pillow cover.

1 Wet the fabric and then follow the manufacturer's instructions for machine dyeing (see page 16).

2 Take out the fabric and leave to dry.

3 Iron the fabric flat and cut a pillow front ⅜ in larger all the way around than the pillow.

4 Cut two pieces for the back of the pillow that are each the same width as the front, but only two-thirds its length. These will overlap one another on the back of the pillow so that when the form is inserted, it will be covered.

5 To prepare the back, machine stitch a 1 in hem along the side of each piece of fabric. This will eventually overlap.

6 Tack or baste the two back pieces together so that the hemmed edges overlap by 4 in. When basted they should be the same size as the front.

7 Sew any decoration, such as the piping spiral, onto the front before sewing it to the back.

8 Pin the front and back together with right sides facing, then machine sew, allowing a ⅜ in seam.

Finished size: 16 sq in

MINIATURE CHEST

THESE SCANDINAVIAN DRAWERS ARE AVAILABLE WORLDWIDE. FOR A MORE FINISHED LOOK WE HAVE TURNED THE DRAWERS AROUND AND ADDED KNOBS. WE CHOSE DYES IN MAUVE AND BLUE.

MATERIALS

Multi-purpose or cold water dyes: blue and mauve
Miniature chest
Wooden knobs (optional)
Screws
Glass jars
Fine sandpaper
Sponge
Rubber gloves
Paintbrush
Clear polyurethane varnish (optional)

INSTRUCTIONS

1. Sand each drawer. Brush off any loose particles.
2. Dissolve each dye in water according to the manufacturer's instructions (see pages 16 and 17).
3. Apply the dissolved dye with a sponge. Sponge in the direction of the grain. Put each drawer to one side and leave to dry before working on the next drawer.
4. Allow to dry thoroughly before applying the next coat. The more colors you add, the deeper the finished color. Remember that the drawers will look darker when wet than when they are dry.
5. Apply dye to the outside surfaces of the chest.
6. Drop the wooden handles into the dye pots and agitate occasionally to get even coverage. When the color is dense enough, remove them and leave to dry.
7. Screw the handles into the drawers. Give each drawer a coat of varnish if you wish to seal it.

GORGEOUS GINGHAM

DYEING GINGHAM TRANSFORMS A UTILITARIAN MATERIAL INTO SOMETHING AS STYLISH AS THESE PILLOWS. CHOOSE COLORS TO COMPLEMENT EACH OTHER OR USE STRIKING OPPOSITES.

MATERIALS

Multi-purpose dyes: red, pink, green and blue
Gingham fabrics
Pillow forms
Salt
Rubber gloves
Iron
Sewing machine and thread
Sewing materials
Ruler

INSTRUCTIONS

Note: You will need enough material to make an envelope-backed pillow cover.

1 Wet the gingham and then follow the manufacturer's instructions for machine dyeing (see page 16).

2 Take out the fabric and leave to dry.

3 Iron the fabric flat and cut a pillow front ⅜ in larger all the way around than the pillow.

4 Cut two pieces for the back of the pillow that are each the same width as the front but only two-thirds its length. These will overlap one another on the back of the pillow so that when the form is inserted, it will be covered.

5 To prepare the back, machine stitch a 1 in hem along the side of each piece of fabric. These will eventually overlap.

6 Tack or baste the two back pieces together so that hemmed edges overlap by 4 in. When basted they should be the same size as the front.

7 Pin the front and back together with right sides facing, then machine sew, allowing a ⅜ in seam.

Finished size: 16 sq in

Alternative ideas
Make a pillow cover with a contrasting frill, as you would a pillowcase, with bow ties to fasten, or stamp a design onto the lighter-colored gingham squares.

WOOLEN MAT

THIS MAT IS MADE FROM AN OLD, CHILD'S BLANKET WHICH HAD SHRUNK AND SLIGHTLY FELTED. IT WAS DYED YELLOW AND DECORATED IN BRIGHT SQUARES OF DYED WOOLS.

MATERIALS

Multi-purpose dyes: pink, green, blue and red
Small woolen blanket
2 sq yds woolen fabric
Salt
Rubber gloves
Fabric glue
Ruler
Scissors

INSTRUCTIONS

1. Cut the woolen fabric into lengths 6 in wide. If you are dyeing in a washing machine there will be some shrinkage and the colors will be softer than if dyeing in a sink or on the stove top.
2. Machine dye the fabric according to the manufacturer's instructions (see page 16). Leave to dry.
3. Measure and cut the pieces into 6 in squares.
4. Cut some pieces into 1¾ x 2⅜ in rectangles.
5. Using fabric glue, stick different colored rectangles onto the squares. Arrange the squares evenly on the background and glue in place.

Finished size: 39½ x 30 in

ACCES

SORIES

This section is packed with ideas for dyeing all kinds of small items, from wrapping paper and stationery to interior accessories such as lamps, table linen and storage boxes. Many of the ideas in this chapter would make ideal gifts for friends and family, or they could even be used to jazz up an office. For example, the magazine files and picture frames will personalize the most sophisticated environment.

LOVELY LINEN

THESE VIBRANT PLACE MATS WITH MATCHING NAPKINS COMBINE THE COLORS OF THE MEDITERRANEAN WITH THE SIMPLE STYLE OF IRISH LINEN.

MATERIALS

Multi-purpose dyes: orange, yellow and red suitable for natural fabrics
1½ yds linen (for 4 napkins and place mats)
Salt
Iron
Rubber gloves
Scissors
Ruler

INSTRUCTIONS

1 Machine dye the linen according to the manufacturer's instructions (see page 16).

2 When dry, iron the linen flat.

3 To make the fringe, pull a thread about ⅜ in from the edge of the linen, along the length and along the width.

4 Keep pulling the threads from the outside edge of the mat until you've achieved the desired effect. Sew a line of straight stitches around all 4 sides to stabilize the edge and to prevent the linen from fraying further.

Finished size: napkins 15 sq in
place mats 11 x 16 in

WRAPPING PAPER

NATURAL PAPERS HAVE WONDERFUL TEXTURES BUT SELDOM COME IN VIBRANT COLORS. WITH THE RICH VARIETY OF DYES ON THE MARKET YOU CAN GIVE THIS PAPER AN EXTRA EDGE.

MATERIALS

Multi-purpose or cold water dyes: purple, yellow, red and green
Sheets of textured natural papers
Rubber gloves
Sponge
Newsprint
Adhesive putty

INSTRUCTIONS

1. Lay the paper out on lining paper. Hold in place with small pieces of adhesive putty if necessary. Dip the sponge in dye and in long sweeping movements, apply the color to one face ofthe paper.
2. Leave to dry.
3. When dry, turn over and apply dye to the other side.

Alternative ideas

You could use a color blending effect with the paper, or add a repeating or random pattern with a stamp.

PICTURE FRAMES

INEXPENSIVE SOFT WOOD PICTURE FRAMES CAN BE MADE TO LOOK SPECIAL WITH A COAT OF DYE WHICH STAINS THE WOOD AND EMPHASIZES ITS GRAIN.

MATERIALS

Multi-purpose or cold water dyes: red, green, yellow, orange and blue
Soft wood frames
Glass jars
Methylated spirits (optional)
Fine sandpaper
Sponge
Rubber gloves
Paintbrush
Clear polyurethane varnish (optional)

INSTRUCTIONS

1. Sand each frame and brush off any dust.
2. Dissolve each dye in water according to the manufacturer's instructions (see pages 16 and 17). If you wish to have a deeper color, mix half water and half methylated spirits. The spirit dissolves in the air, leaving a much deeper color.
3. Apply the dissolved dye to the frame with a sponge. Work in the direction of the grain.
4. Allow to dry thoroughly before applying the next coat.
5. Give each frame a coat of varnish if you wish to seal it.

STORAGE BOXES

THESE BOXES SHOW HOW EVEN CARDBOARD CAN BE DYED SUCCESSFULLY. SMALL, NARROW BOXES COLORED TO YOUR TASTE ARE IDEAL FOR GIFT-WRAPPING SMALL ITEMS SUCH AS GLOVES, TIGHTS AND STOCKINGS OR EVEN T-SHIRTS AND SHIRTS.

MATERIALS

Multi-purpose or cold water dyes: red, pink, blue and green
Cardboard boxes
Glass jars
Rubber gloves
Sponge or large soft brush
Paintbrush
Newsprint

INSTRUCTIONS

1. Remove the lids from the box bases and lay them out on the newsprint.
2. Dip the sponge into the dye and apply the color to one surface of the lid and base. The sponge or brushstrokes should only go in one direction.
3. Leave to dry. When dry, turn over and apply dye to the other side.
4. You will need to touch up the corners using a paintbrush dipped in dye.

GINGHAM TABLECLOTH

GINGHAM AND CHECK GIVE A GOOD BASE FOR DYEING FABRICS. THE BLACK CHECK HERE CONTRASTS WELL WITH THE YELLOW.

MATERIALS

Multi-purpose dye: yellow
6 pieces white cotton fabric each 19 in square
1 piece black-and-white check fabric 45 x 67 in
black cotton fabric 45 x 67 in to edge the tablecloth
1 yd check fabric to make into bias strips to edge the napkins
Salt
Iron
Rubber gloves
Scissors

INSTRUCTIONS

1. Cut two pieces of black fabric 5 x 67 in. Cut two more pieces of black fabric 46 x 5 in.
2. Fold the pieces of fabric lengthwise and press. Use these strips to edge the tablecloth so the fold is on the outside edge and the seams where the bound edge joins onto the cloth.
3. Cut bias strips with the 1 yd piece of check fabric and use them to bind the edge of the napkins.
4. Wet the napkins and cloth thoroughly in water. Then machine dye, following the manufacturer's instructions (see page 16).
5. Remove, allow to dry and iron flat.

PAPER & ENVELOPES

THE TEXTURE OF NATURAL PAPERS AND ENVELOPES IS VERY STYLISH AND BY DYEING THEM YOU CAN CREATE UNIQUE STATIONERY. CHOOSE DYES TO COMPLEMENT ONE ANOTHER OR STRONG, CONTRASTING COLORS.

MATERIALS

Multi-purpose or cold water dyes: blues, pinks, purples and greens
Natural papers and envelopes
Glass jars
Rubber gloves
Sponge or large soft brush
Newsprint

INSTRUCTIONS

1. Mix the dyes according to the manufacturer's instructions (see pages 16 and 17).
2. Lay the papers and envelopes out on lining paper. Dip the sponge or brush in dye and apply the color to one surface of the papers and envelopes. Make the sponge or brushstrokes go in one direction.
3. Leave to dry. When dry, turn over and apply dye to the other side.
4. In the case of the envelopes paint the flap and the back separately.
5. You may need to press the paper and envelopes below a pile of books before using them.

LAVISH LAMPSHADES

LAMPSHADES COME IN A VARIETY OF FABRICS. THESE ARE MADE FROM PAPER. PAINTING THEM WITH DYES MUST BE THE EASIEST TRANSFORMATION EVER MADE.

MATERIALS

Multi-purpose or cold water dyes: yellows, pink, red and blue
Lampshades
Glass jars
Rubber gloves
Sponge

INSTRUCTIONS

1. Mix up the dyes according to the manufacturer's instructions (see pages 16 and 17).
2. Dip an ordinary domestic sponge in dye and apply the color using long, sweeping movements.
3. You may get a little streaking on the first coat, so leave to dry and add more coats until the color is to the depth you desire.

BOX FILES

THESE FILES ARE USUALLY MADE FROM CARDBOARD, BUT HAVING FOUND SOME MADE FROM SOFT WOOD I REALIZED THEY WOULD DYE VERY EFFECTIVELY AND ADD AN EXOTIC TOUCH TO STATIONERY STORAGE.

MATERIALS

Multi-purpose or cold water dyes: pink, red and blue
Soft wood box files
Glass jars
Rubber gloves
Paintbrush
Sponge
Sandpaper
Clear polyurethane varnish (optional)

INSTRUCTIONS

1. Sand the boxes, taking care to get into all the corners (especially if glue has been spilt on the box from when it was made, as the dye will not take over glue). Brush away all dust.
2. Mix up the dyes according to the manufacturer's instructions (see pages 16 and 17).
3. Using a sponge, apply the dye to the outside of the file. Use a paintbrush to touch up inaccessible corners. Leave to dry completely.
4. Turn the box file upside-down and paint the dye on the underside.
5. Apply the dye to the inside.
6. If the color is not deep enough, go over the box again.
7. Apply a coat of polyurethane varnish if you wish to seal it.

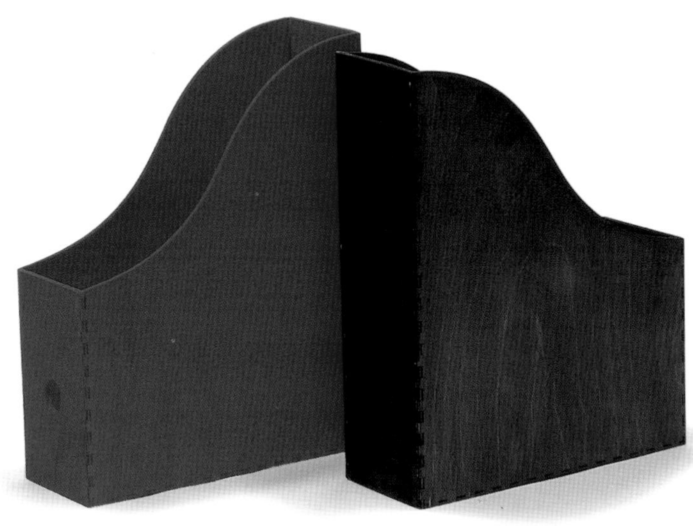

RIT®
COLOR CHART

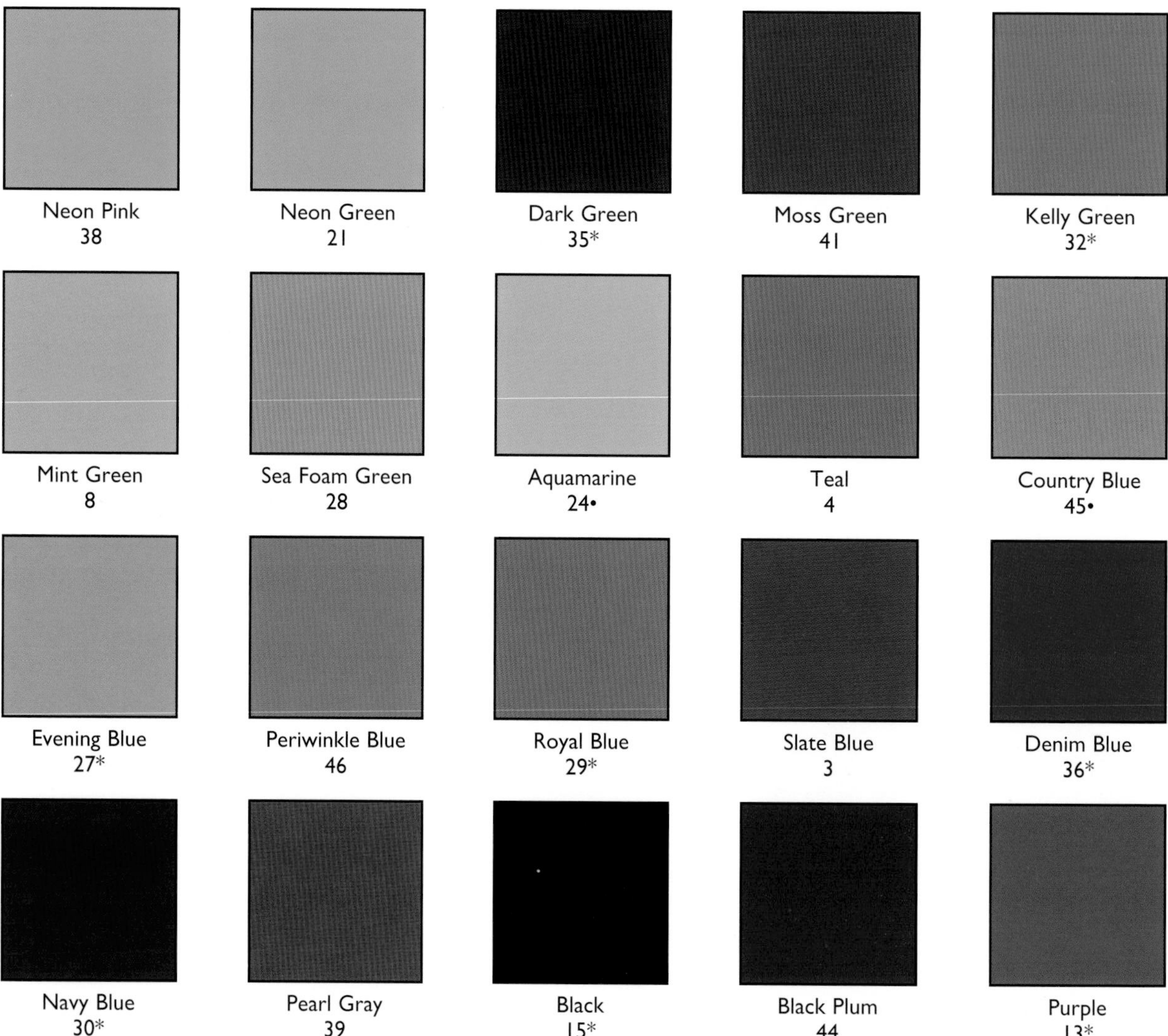

Neon Pink
38
Neon Green
21
Dark Green
35*
Moss Green
41
Kelly Green
32*
Mint Green
8
Sea Foam Green
28
Aquamarine
24•
Teal
4
Country Blue
45•
Evening Blue
27*
Periwinkle Blue
46
Royal Blue
29*
Slate Blue
3
Denim Blue
36*
Navy Blue
30*
Pearl Gray
39
Black
15*
Black Plum
44
Purple
13*

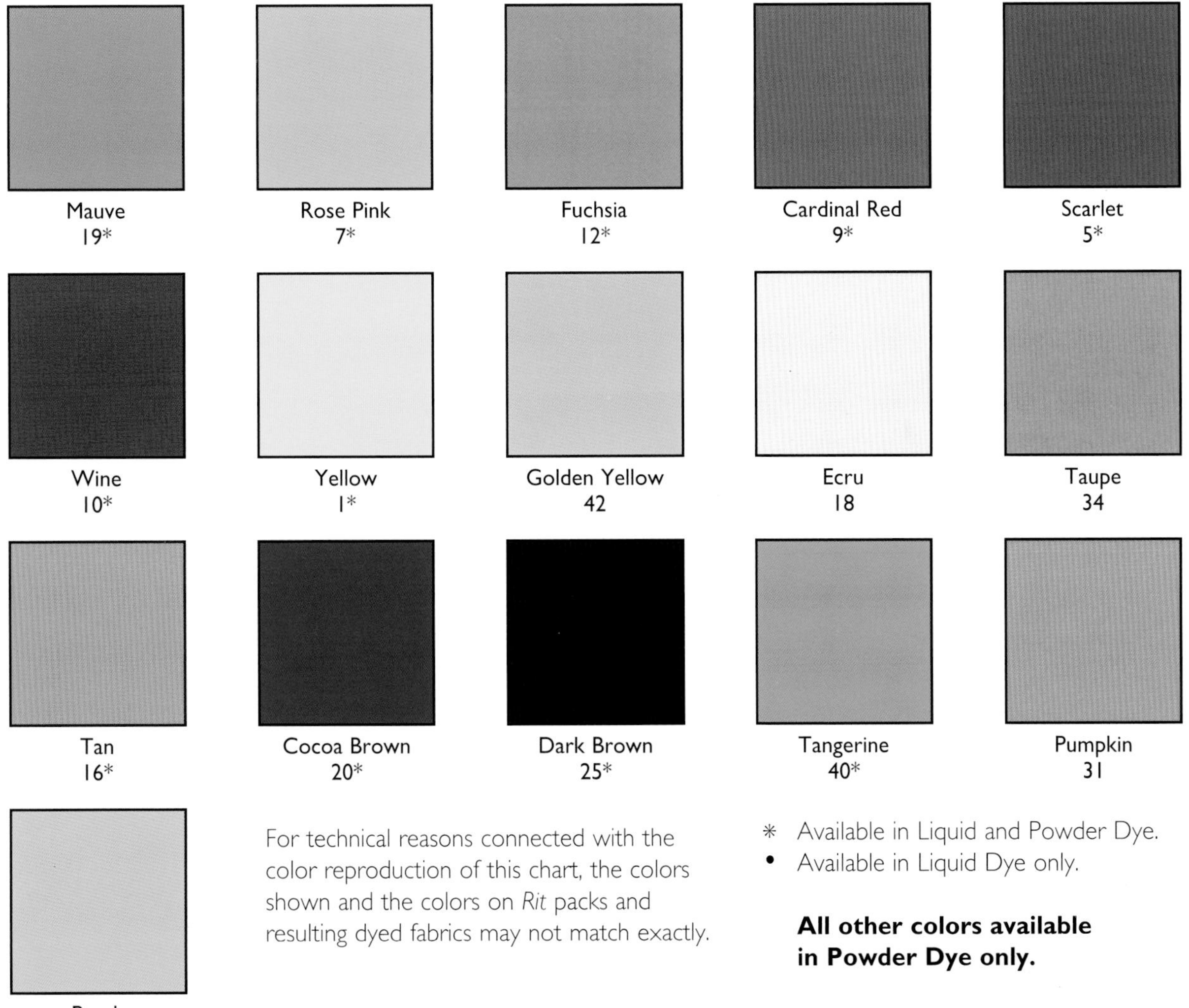

For technical reasons connected with the color reproduction of this chart, the colors shown and the colors on *Rit* packs and resulting dyed fabrics may not match exactly.

* Available in Liquid and Powder Dye.
• Available in Liquid Dye only.

All other colors available in Powder Dye only.

RIT® COVERING GUIDE

THE COLORS ILLUSTRATED ON THE *RIT* PACKAGES AND COLOR CHART REPRESENT THE COLORS OBTAINABLE ON WHITE OR NEAR-WHITE FABRICS. LIGHT *RIT* COLORS, SUCH AS YELLOW, ECRU, OR EVENING BLUE, ARE MOST SATISFACTORY ON WHITE FABRICS IN ORDER TO ACHIEVE TRUE COLORS.

f old color is:	It can be covered with the following *Rit* Dye colors:
Yellow (light)	Scarlet, Tangerine, Cocoa Brown, Dark Brown, Dark Green, Cardinal Red, Wine, Charcoal Gray and Black
Peach, Light Orange, Light Pink	Scarlet, Cardinal Red, Fuchsia, Royal Blue, Cocoa Brown, Tangerine, Wine, Dark Green, Navy Blue and Black
Orange (bright or dark)	Scarlet, Dark Brown and Black
Pink (medium or dark)	Fuchsia, Purple, Wine, Scarlet, Cardinal Red, Cocoa Brown, Dark Brown and Black
Orchid or Lavender	Purple, Wine, Dark Brown, Navy Blue and Black
Bright Red	Wine and Black
Purple	Black
Blue or Turquoise (light)	Royal Blue, Denim Blue, Aquamarine, Purple, Wine, Dark Green, Dark Brown, Navy Blue and Black
Aqua (medium or dark)	Dark Green, Navy Blue and Black
Blue (medium)	Denim Blue, Navy Blue and Black
Green (light)	Royal Blue, Aquamarine, Kelly Green, Dark Green, Dark Brown, Wine, Navy Blue and Black
Chartreuse (light)	Aquamarine, Dark Green, Dark Brown, Wine, Charcoal Gray and Black
Chartreuse (dark)	Dark Green and Black
Green (dark)	Black
Gold (light)	Dark Brown, Dark Green, Cocoa Brown and Black

LIST OF SUPPLIERS

RIT® DYE
RIT® CONSUMER AFFAIRS
P.O. BOX 21070
DEPT. OP-1
INDIANAPOLIS, IN 46221
Tel: 1-317-231-8044
Dye, fabric treatment products, information on dyeing, dye-craft ideas

CERULEAN BLUE LTD.
PO BOX 21168
SEATTLE, WA 98111-3168
Tel: 1-206 323 8600
(Adjustable fabric frame, dye, paints, brushes)

DICK BLICK ART MATERIALS
P.O. BOX 1267
GALESBURG, IL 61402-1267
Tel: 1-800-447-8192
Art supplies, dye, chemicals

EARTH GUILD
33 HAYWOOD ST. DEPT FA
ASHEVILLE, NC 28801
Tel: 1-800-327-8448
Dye, chemicals, fabric paint

GLAD CREATIONS
3400 BLOOMINGTON AVENUE SOUTH
MINNEAPOLIS, MN 55407
Tel: 1-612-724-1079
Fabrics

RUPERT, GIBBON & SPIDER, INC.
P.O. BOX 425
HEALDSBURG, CA 95448
Tel: 1-800-442-0455
Dye, chemicals, fabric, supplies

STAPLES, INC.
8 TECHNOLOGY DRIVE
PO BOX 1020
WESTBOROUGH, MA 01581
Tel: 1-800-333-3330
Adhesive putty

SILK ETCETERA INTERNATIONAL
P.O. BOX 5102
SANTA CRUZ, CA 95063
Tel: 408-476-6656
Fabric, supplies

TESTFABRICS, INC.
P.O. BOX 420
MIDDLESEX, NJ 08846
Tel: 1-908-469-6446
Fabrics

THAI SILKS
252 STATE STREET
LOS ALTOS, CA 94022
Tel: 1-415-948-8611
Fabrics

QUALIN INTERNATIONAL, INC.
PO BOX 31145-T
SAN FRANCISCO, CA 94131
Tel: 1-415 333-8500
Fabrics